THE PUPPY PLACE

Don't miss any of these other stories by Ellen Miles!

THE PUPPY PLACE

JAKE

**ELLEN
MILES**

SCHOLASTIC INC.

For Maria and Luna
Many thanks to my horse specialists, Pat and Jamie

Copyright © 2017 by Ellen Miles
Cover art by Tim O'Brien
Original cover design by Steve Scott

All rights reserved. Published by Scholastic Inc., *Publishers since 1920.* SCHOLASTIC and associated logos are trademarks and/or registered trademarks of Scholastic Inc.

The publisher does not have any control over and does not assume any responsibility for author or third-party websites or their content.

No part of this publication may be reproduced, stored in a retrieval system, or transmitted in any form or by any means, electronic, mechanical, photocopying, recording, or otherwise, without written permission of the publisher. For information regarding permission, write to Scholastic Inc., Attention: Permissions Department, 557 Broadway, New York, NY 10012.

ISBN 978-1-338-06927-3

10 9 8 7 6 5 4 3 2   17 18 19 20 21

Printed in the U.S.A.   40

First printing 2017

CHAPTER ONE

"I don't know," said Lizzie. "I guess I'm still not getting it, but how can it be any fun when all you do is work?"

"Trust me," said Maria. "It's so much fun. More fun than Disneyland. More fun than Halloween."

Lizzie raised an eyebrow. Sometimes Maria exaggerated. Could horse camp really be better than Halloween?

Lizzie Peterson and her best friend, Maria Santiago, were on their way to Appletree Farm, a horse camp in the country. Maria had been to Appletree twice before, once for an introductory weekend and once for a whole ten-day session in the summer. Maria was horse-crazy and had been riding since she was three years old.

Lizzie, on the other hand, was not quite so horse-crazy. Until recently, in fact, she had pretty much been afraid of horses. They were big, they were unpredictable, and their hooves and teeth were huge. Who wouldn't be afraid? Now that she had taken a bunch of lessons at the stable where Maria usually rode, Lizzie felt a lot less nervous around horses, but she still liked dogs better.

Lizzie was even crazier about dogs than Maria was about horses. Her goal in life was to spend as much time as possible around dogs. She helped out at her aunt Amanda's doggy day care. She volunteered at Caring Paws, the local animal shelter. She had even started her own dog-walking business (Maria was one of her partners). That would have been plenty for most people. Not for Lizzie.

She had also convinced her parents that their family (her dad, a firefighter; her mom, a newspaper reporter; and her two younger brothers, Charles and the Bean) should become a foster family for puppies. They had tried it, and everybody liked it (even Mom, who was really more of a cat person), so they had kept on doing it.

By now everybody in Littleton knew that the Petersons were the people to turn to if you heard about a puppy in need of help. The Petersons had taken care of dozens of puppies, keeping each one until they had found it the perfect forever home. Lizzie loved getting to know the puppies and figuring out what kind of home would be best for each one, depending on its personality. She knew how important it was to make a good match: people who hated exercise should not adopt a dog who loved and needed a lot of it, for example.

The best match ever was the one they'd made

for Buddy, a sweet brown-and-white mixed-breed puppy the Petersons had fostered — then ended up adopting. Buddy was a part of their family now, and Lizzie loved him more than anything in the world.

"Buddy face," said Maria now, as they drove along a bumpy country road. "You're thinking about him, aren't you?" She could always tell when Lizzie was thinking about her puppy. "You've got that certain smile."

Maria's father glanced in the rearview mirror and grinned at Lizzie. "Even I can tell when you're thinking about Buddy," he said. "You sure do love that puppy, don't you?"

Mr. Santiago was such a good sport. When the owners of Appletree Farm had invited Maria and a friend to join them for their introduction-to-camp weekend, he had agreed on very short notice to drive the girls there. It was a three-hour trip, but he didn't seem to mind. "I've been wishing for a drive in the country," he said. "I love it at this time of year, when the leaves are just bursting out on the trees."

Lizzie loved early spring, too. It wasn't too hot yet, there was always a breeze, and everything was green, green, green. She smiled, thinking about how Buddy loved to roll around in the bright new grass, scratching his back for the first time after a long winter.

"Buddy face again!" said Maria. "Time to start thinking about horses. I wonder if I'll get Raven for the weekend. I had him last summer, and he's the best. He doesn't try to pull funny tricks like some of the other ponies." She looked at Lizzie. "And for you . . . I bet they'll put you on Smokey. He's such a sweetie. He's perfect for —" She stopped.

"Perfect for somebody who doesn't know what she's doing?" Lizzie asked.

Maria laughed. "No, of course not. You've gotten so good. You know how to trot now, and post, and step in your irons."

"It's funny that a few months ago I barely even knew what any of those things meant," said Lizzie. Now she knew that trotting was the next speed after a walk (before cantering and galloping), that "posting" meant the way a rider rose and fell in tune with her horse's gait, and that "stepping in her irons" meant using her feet in her stirrups in the most effective way.

"The best part of that is you'll probably get to go on trail rides," said Maria. "Jean won't let anybody go until she's tested them on the basics."

Jean. Lizzie had never met her, but she was already a little afraid of her. From what Maria had told her, she knew that one of the owners of Appletree Farm was very strict about certain things, like the barn rules and the way her horses were cared for. Kathy, the woman who ran the stable where Maria and Lizzie usually took lessons, was like that, too. It wasn't easy to please either of them, but once they knew you were serious about riding, they could teach you a lot.

Lizzie wondered what Jean would think of her. Lizzie was not exactly serious about riding, even though she had enjoyed getting better at it. If only she could keep from making easy mistakes, like dropping a clanging bucket in the stable and scaring the horses. Kathy always had to remind Lizzie to move carefully in the stable and to think before she acted. Lizzie resolved to be very careful around Jean. She did not want to get the "fisheye," which was what Maria said all the campers called it when Jean looked at you a certain way.

"Don't worry," said Maria, as if she was still reading Lizzie's thoughts. "If you're lucky, you'll get Sally for your lessons."

Sally was Appletree's other owner. She was Jean's cousin, but according to Maria, you'd never guess they were related. Sally was warm and smiley and liked to hug and was always encouraging. Lizzie hoped to spend a lot more time with Sally than with Jean.

Lizzie also hoped she would learn to love mucking out messy stalls, shoveling in clean new bedding, lugging buckets of water and oats, brushing and washing her horse's coat and combing its mane, picking stuff out of its hooves, and doing all the other things Maria had told her that campers were required to do every day.

At Kathy's, Lizzie had learned a little bit about how to take care of horses, but the people who went there for lessons were not expected to do everything, the way campers at Appletree were. "I still just can't believe it'll be fun," she said one more time as Mr. Santiago turned down a long, bumpy gravel driveway. There was the sign for Appletree Farm. There were the pastures full of horses, the riding rings, the big red barn. They had arrived, and for better or worse Lizzie was going to be spending the weekend completely focused on horses.

Or was she?

"Look!" she said as they pulled up in front of a big red barn. "It's a puppy!"

CHAPTER TWO

"You didn't tell me there was a puppy here," said Lizzie. As soon as Mr. Santiago stopped the car, Lizzie unsnapped her seat belt and leapt out. She held out her hand to the gangly puppy. He had a short shiny white coat with lots of brown speckles and spots, gorgeous long brown ears, and beautiful golden eyes. He was muscular and thin, like a long-distance runner, with big chunky paws and a broad chest. "A German shorthaired pointer," she added. Lizzie recognized him right away from her "Dog Breeds of the World" poster. "You know I've always wanted to meet one. Why didn't you tell me?"

"I didn't know," said Maria. "He wasn't here last year."

"But he's not a baby," said Lizzie as she petted the puppy's velvety-soft nose. "He must be at least a year old." The dog had come right over when she crouched down and called him, and now he pushed his nose against her hand, eager for affection. Then he jumped up and put his paws on Lizzie's chest.

Finally! Some attention. Usually everybody's just interested in the horses.

"Uh-uh!" said Lizzie. As cute as he was, the puppy had to learn that jumping up was never okay. She staggered to get her balance, then stood up tall and turned her back on the puppy. It killed her to do it; she hated taking her eyes off his incredible cuteness. But she knew that the best way to train a dog not to jump up was to ignore him when he did and reward him when he didn't.

Lizzie peered over her shoulder and saw that the puppy had sat back on his haunches and was looking up at her with big, plaintive eyes.

Don't you like me anymore? I thought we were friends.

As soon as she saw that he was sitting, Lizzie spun around and knelt to pet the puppy's head. "Good boy," she said. "No jumping." She fished around for a treat in her pocket and found one of Buddy's freeze-dried liver snacks. She gave it to the puppy fast, before he could jump up again.

Maria knelt down, too. The puppy wagged his stumpy tail and snuffled at her hand when she petted him. "They must have adopted him since I was last here," she said.

"Oh, no, we haven't," said someone behind them.

Lizzie turned to see a tall woman in jeans and riding boots. Her brown hair was pulled back in a ponytail, and her lean face was suntanned and stern.

Jean. It had to be Jean.

"He's a stray," said the woman. "Showed up here about three weeks ago. My cousin has been calling him Jake and she thinks we should keep him, but that's not going to happen. A pointer is not the right kind of dog to have around a stable. Too excitable. The horses need a calm environment." She strode toward Mr. Santiago and offered her hand for a shake. "Good to see you again," she said.

Mr. Santiago smiled. "Good to see you, too, Jean."

So it *was* Jean. Lizzie had been right.

"We are really grateful for this opportunity," said Mr. Santiago, nudging Maria with his toe.

Maria stood up quickly, dusted off her hands, and smiled at Jean. "We are. I mean, thanks very much for inviting me and —" She turned to Lizzie. "This is Lizzie Peterson, my best friend."

Lizzie stood up, too. She was already dreaming about taking Jake home with her when the weekend was over. She could tell instantly that he was a very cool puppy. Maybe he was excitable, but he was also friendly. And judging by the way he looked, she could tell he was probably a real athlete. Maybe he would enjoy doing agility, or maybe she could find out where to take him for training as a bird dog. That was what pointers were bred for, after all. "So Jake needs a real home somewhere?" she asked. "My family fosters puppies. Maybe we could —"

Jean just smiled a tight little smile. "Nice to meet you, too," she said. Then the smile disappeared. "No time for puppies now," she said. "We've got chores to do."

Lizzie held back a groan. The work was already starting. All she really wanted to do was play with Jake.

"Put your stuff on the porch," said Jean. "You can bring it upstairs to the dorm later. Right now there are horses waiting to meet you." Without a backward glance, she headed into the barn.

Maria smiled at Lizzie. "Here we go," she said.

"Here we go," repeated Lizzie. She petted Jake one more time, sliding her hand down his long silky-soft ears. "I'll see you later," she whispered to him. He licked her hand once, then scampered off toward the barn. Lizzie and Maria grabbed their backpacks and sleeping bags out of the trunk of the car, and Maria hugged her dad good-bye.

"See you Monday afternoon," he said. He gave Lizzie a hug, too. "If I know you, we may have an extra rider in the car on the way back. Don't forget to check with your parents before you bring a puppy home!"

Lizzie laughed. "I know, I know," she said. She slung her backpack over her shoulder and followed Maria to the old white farmhouse across the road. They tossed their things onto one of the rockers that lined the long open porch. Then Maria led Lizzie back to the barn.

The look and smell were familiar to Lizzie right away. This was a lot like Kathy's barn, dark and sweet-smelling, with an aisle down the middle and horse stalls on either side. Each stall had a nameplate, and Lizzie read the names to herself as she walked behind Maria. "'Rocco,' 'Boots,' 'Misty,' 'Chester,'" she read.

Some of the horses swung their heads over their stall doors, nickering softly as the girls walked by. Maria stopped to pet Rocco and Misty, who nodded their heads and nuzzled her pockets for carrots as she moved close. Lizzie wasn't ready to pat an unfamiliar horse. She knew some horses could be nippy or pushy.

A group of girls stood at the far end of the barn in a loose semicircle around Jean. "Some of you have been here before, so you know the stable rules," she was saying. "I expect you to help the new girls learn how we do things here." She introduced a college-age girl named Candace, who had brought over a whiteboard with BARN RULES written at the top. "Candace helps out with whatever needs doing around here," Jean said. "If you have any questions or problems, she can help you." Then Jean began to go over what was written on the board. "No unsupervised riding allowed," she said. "None. Absolutely never. That's rule number one." She peered around at all the girls to see if they were paying attention.

Lizzie nodded. She got it. She really did. No riding without supervision. Not that she'd be likely to, anyway. She needed all the help she could get, and she knew she was not nearly ready to be riding on her own.

"'All tack cleaned and inspected before tacking up,'" read Jean next. "Everybody knows what tacking up is, right?"

Lizzie nodded again, along with everyone else. Tacking up was when you put on all the things a horse needed to wear when you were going to ride it: a saddle pad, the saddle, the girth —

which was like a belt that went around the horse's stomach — and the bridle, which had a bit to go in the horse's mouth and reins for the rider to hold.

"Why do we clean tack?" asked Jean, raising one eyebrow. "Maria?"

"Because horses sweat," said Maria. "They sweat when they're working, and their tack is like our clothes. We wash our clothes after we sweat in them."

Jean nodded and gave Maria a tight-lipped smile. "And why do we inspect our tack?" She turned her gaze on Lizzie. "Lizzie?"

"Um," said Lizzie. For a second, her head was completely empty. It was because of the way Jean was looking at her. She felt Maria reach out and grasp her hand, and that seemed to bring her brain back. "Because something might be worn out or about to break, and that could be danger-ous?" she said.

Jean nodded. "Exactly. Very good." She smiled that tight smile at Lizzie, and Lizzie felt like she might faint. *Phew.* She had passed her first test.

CHAPTER THREE

Lizzie relaxed as Jean continued talking. First of all, she already knew most of these rules from being at Kathy's barn. Second, she had been tested by Jean and had come out looking good. And third, Jake had just sidled up next to her and was pushing his warm, wet nose into her hand, looking for pats.

"Jake," she whispered. "Hey, pal." She scratched between his ears as she listened to Jean. Jake pushed against her hand.

You're the only one giving me attention around here. More, more!

Lizzie smiled. Dogs always knew who to come to for attention and affection. Jake knew a dog lover when he smelled one. Then Jake put a chunky paw onto Lizzie's knee. "Uh-uh," Lizzie said. She was a dog lover, but she didn't put up with that. It was cute when a tiny puppy pawed at you, but it wasn't so adorable when the puppy grew up to be a big dog. Lizzie put Jake's paw back on the stable floor. "Good boy," she whispered. She turned her attention back to Jean.

"The thing about horses is that they're always thinking," Jean was saying. "So we have to think, too — just to stay one step ahead of them. Remember, also, that horses are prey animals. That means they are always on the lookout for some other animal that might try to chase or eat them." She turned to pet the nose of a large chestnut-brown horse whose head hung over his stall door. "Right, Chester?" she asked. "That's why we are always gentle with our horses, why we don't startle them, why we are always aware that they might be startled by something out of our control. Like on a trail ride, we might see a deer or even a coyote, or a branch might fall out of a tree. The horses will react to that, and you'll need to know how to react to your horse. We'll talk more about that before our trail ride."

Jean went on, and Lizzie listened. But Jake needed her attention, too. He leaned against her leg as she scratched harder between his ears. She began running her hand down his back so she could scratch there, too. Jake wriggled with delight. Lizzie stroked his ears, scratched his head again, scratched his back. Jake loved it all.

"All right, then. I think that's it for the rules

today," Jean said finally. "Are you girls ready to meet the horses you'll be in charge of for the weekend?"

Everybody nodded and said yes, but they said it quietly. They knew better than to let out a loud cheer. Shouting in the stable was a definite no-no.

"Sally? Do you have the list?" Jean asked.

A woman bustled down the aisle, holding a clipboard high. "Here it is, just in time!" she said.

Sally looked like she'd be just as nice as Lizzie had imagined. She had a rosy face with a wide smile, and her graying hair was in two long thick braids.

"Sorry I'm late," she said. "One of the sheep decided to have her lambs way out in the far pasture this morning. Twins! So cute."

"Sally loves her sheep," Maria whispered to Lizzie, "even though they're always doing silly things."

Jean took the clipboard, pulled a pair of reading glasses out of her pocket, and put them on. Then she began to read. "Okay, we've got Kate paired with Misty," she began.

Lizzie heard a tiny cheer behind her and turned to see a red-haired girl grinning and pumping her fist.

Jean frowned, peering over the top of her reading glasses, and the red-haired girl put her hands over her mouth. "Oops," she said.

Jean smiled. "It's okay. I know some of you have formed some strong relationships with certain horses. That's a good thing. Let's just keep the cheering to a minimum." She looked down at the clipboard again. "Speaking of strong relationships . . . Maria, you'll be with Raven again."

Maria didn't cheer out loud, but she reached out and squeezed Lizzie's hand so hard that Lizzie almost squeaked.

"Yay," Maria whispered.

"And, Lizzie, we've got you with Smokey," Jean said.

Lizzie and Maria grinned at each other, and this time Lizzie squeezed Maria's hand. If her friend thought that Smokey was a good horse for her, Lizzie was sure she was right.

Once all the names were read out loud, Jean told the girls to go say hello to their horses. "We won't be riding until tomorrow. So just get acquainted for now, and then we'll head inside for dinner and some more orientation to camp." She passed out carrots from a burlap bag that Sally had dragged down the aisle. "These should help you make friends."

Maria led Lizzie up the aisle. "It's perfect," she said. "Raven and Smokey are right next to each other." She pointed to two stalls on the right. A black horse was in one, a gray spotted horse in the other.

Lizzie could guess which one was Smokey. His dappled gray coat looked just like swirling smoke. When he saw them coming, he put his big head out of the stall and tossed it around a bit. Lizzie took a deep breath, told herself to be brave and confident, and marched right up to the stall. "Hi, Smokey," she said, holding up the carrot on her flat palm, the way she'd learned at Kathy's.

Smokey pulled away from her hand.

"Lizzie!" Maria hissed. "What are you doing? Didn't you hear what Jean just said? It's one of the most basic barn rules."

Lizzie shook her head, speechless. What had she done?

"Do not stand directly in front of a horse's face." Lizzie did not have to turn around to know that it was Jean behind her, quoting the rule. She felt her whole body turn hot, then cold, then hot again.

"You heard me say it, didn't you?" Jean asked when Lizzie did turn around. Jean stood with her arms crossed, and the way she looked at Lizzie — well, Lizzie knew right away that she was getting the famous fisheye.

CHAPTER FOUR

"I — I —" It seemed Lizzie couldn't get the words out. Then she felt something very familiar — a cool wet nose touching her hand. She looked down to see Jake pushing into her. He tried to jump up, but she turned her back on him and he sat down. Then he pushed his nose into her hand again.

"It's that dog, I'm telling you," said Jean. But this time she wasn't speaking to Lizzie. She was talking to Sally, who had also arrived quickly at Smokey's stall. "See? He's a distraction, and a pest, and just . . . not good for a stable." She shook her head.

"It's not Jake's fault I wasn't listening," said Lizzie. "It's mine. I thought I already knew the rules. I'm really sorry."

"Smokey's the one you should apologize to," said Jean. "He's the sweetest pony in the world, wouldn't hurt a fly, but he is shy around strangers. He needs a little time to get to know you. That's why we have the rule."

Lizzie knew that every horse had his own personality, just like every dog did. She knew dogs who would have acted exactly the same way if she'd tried to pet them without letting them sniff her hand first. If you saw a dog pull away like that, you could guess that he was a little shy and you had frightened him. She felt terrible and turned to tell Smokey she was sorry. His head was hanging over the stall door again — *way* over. He leaned far down, touching noses with Jake, who was stretching his neck way up to say hi.

"Whoa!" Lizzie said. "They're friends!" It was unmistakable. Jake and Smokey were besties. Jake wagged his tail as he snuffled at the horse. Smokey snuffled gently, too, and blew air out of his nose.

Sally laughed. "They sure are," she said. She slung an arm over Lizzie's shoulders. "You can't miss it, can you?" She grinned at her cousin. "See? Let's not be in such a hurry to get rid of Smokey's new friend. Poor Jake. He's already lost one home by not measuring up. I think he wants to please us. We just have to let him know what we expect."

Jean shook her head and strode off up the aisle.

"What do you mean, he lost a home?" Lizzie asked Sally. She knew she should probably keep her mouth shut right now, but she couldn't help asking.

"Somebody left him on the side of the road," said Sally. "They probably thought they were

31

doing the right thing by dropping him off at the farm. Everybody knows that we're animal people here."

Jake and Smokey were still touching noses. Lizzie loved watching the two of them together. This friendship was really something special.

"I think you're an animal person, too," Sally said quietly, putting her hand on Lizzie's shoulder. "I saw how you handled it when Jake tried to jump up on you. You know what you're doing around dogs."

Lizzie felt herself blushing. "Maybe," she said. "But I still have a lot to learn. And I really have a lot to learn about horses."

Sally smiled and nodded. "That's what's so wonderful about working with animals. There's always more to learn. I've been riding and training horses since I was your age — maybe even younger — but I still learn new things all the time." She clucked her tongue and Smokey swung his head up. "Hey there, Mr. Smokes," she said, petting his nose and giving him a scratch between the ears. "You're going to love this girl once you get to know her."

"I'm Lizzie." Lizzie realized that she had not introduced herself to Sally yet.

"I figured," said Sally. "There aren't that many new faces here this weekend, and I saw you with Maria. We're happy to have you."

Lizzie raised her eyebrows. Jean sure didn't seem so happy.

Sally smiled. "I know some of us may not always act that way, but believe me. You're very welcome at Appletree Farm. Now let's get to know this horse." She patted the stall door. "Come on up, but just approach from the side so he can get a good look at you. Horses do not like it when they aren't sure who's near them."

Lizzie moved slowly and carefully toward Smokey. Jake sidled along next to her.

I'm not going anywhere, especially not if you stick around this guy. He's my pal.

"Smokey loves carrots," Sally prompted Lizzie.

Lizzie remembered the carrot in her hand and offered it again, moving her hand slowly toward Smokey's mouth. This time he took it, his big lips brushing her palm as he accepted the treat. He chomped away happily, stomping one foot and whisking his long white tail as if to say, "Finally, I got my carrot!" Then he stretched out his neck and nuzzled Lizzie's shoulder, then stretched it even further to push at her jacket pocket.

"He wants another one!" said Lizzie.

"See? You speak horse," said Sally. "I knew you were an animal person." She handed Lizzie another carrot, and Lizzie gave it to Smokey. This time she petted his big long jaw as he chomped. She could feel his huge teeth grinding the carrot to bits — but she wasn't scared. She wasn't scared at all. Smokey was a sweetheart; she could tell.

So was Jake. Lizzie smiled down at the dog, who was still leaning against her leg. Smokey was not the only friend Jake had made at the barn. With luck, maybe Lizzie would be taking Jake home with her when the weekend was over. She might not know a lot about horses, but Lizzie definitely knew how to foster a puppy — especially one as sweet and cute as this one.

CHAPTER FIVE

"That pooch sure has taken a shine to you, Lizzie," said Sally after dinner that night. She and Jean and all the campers were spread out on the big shabby couches in the farmhouse common room. There was a fire in the huge stone fireplace, and Lizzie was snuggled cozily in a corner of one couch with Jake curled up close beside her. Sally laughed when Lizzie had asked if she should tell Jake to get off the couch. "Dogs have the run of this house," Sally had said. "All furniture is fair game. That's how it's always been, anyway."

"I like Jake, too," said Lizzie now. "He's such a sweet boy." She scratched Jake's head, and he stirred from his nap to look up at her with his happy golden eyes.

I knew I picked you out for a reason.

Maria scratched Jake's other end. "Thanks for the pineapple upside-down cake, Sally," she said. "That was awesome."

"The whole dinner was awesome," said Lizzie.

"Well, maybe that's because everyone helped," said Sally. "I always think food tastes better when you were a part of cooking it."

Lizzie and Maria gave each other a fist bump. "Carrot crew rules!" said Maria. The two friends had peeled and shredded five pounds of carrots for the giant vat of coleslaw Sally wanted to make.

"Cabbage crew is number one!" shouted Nadia.

"No way, no way!" yelled Emma. "Table-setting crew can't be beat."

Lizzie laughed. Horse campers could be really competitive — like during dinner when Jean had gone over the plans for the next morning. When she had asked campers to help her list some of the things they'd be doing, everybody started shouting.

"Fill water buckets!" said Kaila.

"Grain your horse," Emma said. (Lizzie figured that meant you gave your horse some grain. What else could it mean?)

Maria waved her hand as if she was at school. "Remove bunzies."

"Bunzies?" Lizzie stared at Maria. "What are bunzies?" She'd never heard that word before.

At that, everybody in the room started to laugh hysterically while Lizzie just sat there, confused. What was the word? What was the joke? Finally, Maria managed to catch her breath. Her face was bright red. She wiped away a few tears as she explained. "You know, the stuff that comes out after the grain goes in," she said.

Lizzie still didn't get it.

"Horse poops!" crowed Emma, and everybody started to laugh hysterically all over again. This time, Lizzie joined them. "Bunzies" — what a funny word.

What wasn't as funny was all the rest of the chores Jean named, in order. This was how they would spend the next morning:

- Wake up at 7:00
- 7:30–8:00: Breakfast

According to Maria, Sally made the world's best waffles, so maybe that part would be okay. And at least they didn't have to help clean up, like they did after dinner.

- 8:00–10:30: Get ready to ride

Why did it take so long to get ready to ride? That's what Lizzie wondered, until Jean explained it. Getting ready to ride included:

- Graining the horses
- Filling water buckets
- Following the truck outside to spread bales of hay over the fields
- Filling up the outdoor water tank
- Turning out horses

Turning out your horse meant leading it out on a halter. That was going to be a new one for Lizzie. At the stable at home, Kathy had always led their horses out for their lessons.

The list went on and on. As she listened, Lizzie lay back on the couch, wishing she was already in bed. She needed her rest if she was going to be doing all that work!

"Okay. Now that the horses are in the pasture, it's time to clean out the stalls. Yes, that's right: it's time to remove those bunzies," said Jean the next morning. The campers were already hard at work at the tasks she had outlined the night before. She allowed herself a small smile when the girls cracked up. She strode up the stable aisle, nodding as she passed each stall. "When you've cleaned the stalls and put in fresh bedding, then you'll scrub and refill those water buckets, sweep the barn floors, make sure the horse brushes are cleaned and put away . . ."

Lizzie sighed. That wasn't even all of it, she knew. She remembered the other things Jean had listed the night before: cleaning and going over your tack, then finally going to get your horse back out of the pasture, then putting the horse on the crossties (the ropes that crossed the aisle next to each stall) and grooming the horse (that included brushing, combing the horse's mane and tail, and picking out hooves). After that they would tack up, putting on a saddle pad, saddle, and girth. Then they would go put on their own gear: helmets, chaps, gloves.

"Then, finally," Lizzie told Jake as she refilled Smokey's water bucket with fresh cold water, "we get to put the bridle on the horse and lead it out to the ring for our lesson. Then, after our lesson, we do the whole thing all over again, backward. Can you believe how much work it is to take care of a horse?"

Jake snuffled as he put his nose into her hand. The puppy had followed Lizzie everywhere since the moment they met. He had lain under her chair at the dinner table, snoozed on the couch with her, squeezed himself into her tiny cot in the upstairs dorm, and stuck close to her side through breakfast and the beginning of the camp day.

Who cares if we're working or playing? We're together. And my best friend is here, too.

Jake and Smokey had been so happy to see each other when Lizzie and the puppy came into the barn that morning. Smokey let out a loud whinny as soon as he saw Jake padding down the aisle, and Jake's wagging tail was a blur as he touched noses with his big gray friend. Lizzie was beginning to feel guilty about her plan to take Jake home with her when she left camp. This puppy needed a home where he was accepted and loved, but how could she tear him away from his best pal, Smokey?

CHAPTER SIX

"Very nice, Lizzie." Sally nodded approvingly as Lizzie walked Smokey around the riding ring. "You have a natural seat."

Lizzie beamed. Nobody had ever said that to her before. Maybe she could get good at this horse-riding thing after all. She knew that Sally was talking about the way she sat on Smokey and moved with his movements. Lizzie wasn't sure it felt all that natural to her — in fact, she had a feeling that her "seat" was going to be pretty sore by the end of the weekend. Still, the compliment meant a lot.

Smokey nickered and tossed his head. Lizzie

looked ahead and saw Jake standing on his back legs, front paws up on the riding ring's fence. She gave Smokey a gentle squeeze with her legs and a tiny tug on the right rein, to remind him to focus. "Keep going," she said softly to him. "No stopping to see your friend now."

"Candace," Jean called from the other side of the ring, where she was watching Maria trot by. "Get that dog out of here, would you? He's distracting the horses. Put him in the house."

Jean didn't miss anything, Lizzie realized. Her sharp eyes noticed it all. That morning when Lizzie was getting water for Smokey's bucket, Jean had reminded her to scrub it out before she refilled it. She'd also noticed when Lizzie missed picking out one of Smokey's hooves. At least it wasn't just Lizzie. Jean had roamed the aisles, watching everything closely and commenting when any of the girls did anything that wasn't up to her standards.

Still, Lizzie felt like she had done pretty well for her first time getting a horse ready to ride. Maria had helped a lot, reminding her of the next step whenever they finished a task. "Now we go get our tack," she'd told Lizzie once the horses were groomed. "But remember, don't put the bridle on until the very last thing, after you get your own boots and gloves and helmet on."

Lizzie had been pretty impressed with herself when she led Smokey out into the ring, all groomed, tacked up, and ready to ride. She'd learned a lot in just a few hours. And thanks to her lessons at Kathy's, she knew how to climb into her horse's saddle with a leg up from Sally, and how to arrange the reins in her hands. But was she ready for trail riding? That would be up to Sally and Jean, according to Maria.

"They'll check you out on some basic skills," Maria said as she and Lizzie had led their horses out to the ring. "They'll be checking every-body out this morning. Nobody gets to go on a trail ride unless they've shown that they know how to control a horse."

Lizzie knew she had the basic skills. But would Sally and Jean agree? And even if they did, was Lizzie really ready for a trail ride? It sounded exciting and scary at the same time. Riding through the woods would be awesome — but what if the horses got spooked by something and started to gallop all over the place? Lizzie wasn't sure she could hold her "natural seat" if that hap-pened. Maria had said that the trail rides were mellow, mostly walking — but still, out there in the woods almost anything could happen.

"Okay, let's see you take Smokey into a trot now," said Sally.

Lizzie gulped. Riding a walking horse was easy. Trotting was another story. Still, she had been working on her trot at Kathy's and had learned to post — to rise and fall in the saddle, using the strength of her legs to stay with the horse's motion — even at a fast trot. She took a deep breath and let it out. Then she gave Smokey a little nudge with her heels, the signal to speed up. He was ready for it and broke immediately into a trot. Lizzie felt herself jolted around for a moment, but then she recovered her seat and got into rhythm with Smokey's movements.

"Looking good," said Sally as they passed. "Lovely, Lizzie."

"Loosen up on those reins," Jean called from across the ring. "Don't grip so hard."

How did she see everything? Lizzie looked down and realized Jean was right. Her gloved hands were clenched tightly on the reins. She relaxed a bit. That felt better.

"Good," called Jean.

Lizzie grinned. She was doing all right! Even Jean thought so.

When the lesson ended, Sally told the girls to lead their horses down to the river for a drink before they took off their tack and washed them down. "It's hot and dusty today, and they deserve to splash around a little," she said.

She and Jean followed the parade of horses down the well-beaten path that ran behind the barn. Lizzie was proud of the way Smokey followed her as she walked just ahead of him, holding his bridle. But when they got to the river, its clear green water sparkling in the sunshine as it tumbled over rocks, Smokey had ideas of his own. He tugged her toward a spot near a willow tree and nearly pulled her into the water as he lowered his head for a long, slurpy drink.

"Smokey always goes to that spot," said Sally, laughing. "He doesn't like it if anyone else tries to join him there, either." She and Jean sat on a wide rock, talking quietly, as the girls let their horses drink.

Afterward, they paraded back to the barn and began the long process of removing tack and cleaning and grooming the horses. When that was done, they turned the horses out into the pasture, where they could munch on sweet green grass while the girls had their lunch.

Lizzie was starving by the time they sat down at the picnic tables under a blossoming apple tree. The sweet scent of the white petals wafted over her as she reached for a second helping of coleslaw. Jake sat at her feet, probably hoping for a scrap of her cheese sandwich. He had rushed out of the house as soon as the door was opened, straight to Lizzie's side.

Hey, friend! Hey, friend! Hey, friend!

He had tried to jump up on her, but Lizzie had turned her back until he was sitting nicely. He sure was a fast learner. "I know we won't have any trouble finding you a home," she said to him. "If I get to foster you, that is."

Now Jean stood up and clapped her hands for attention. "You all looked terrific in the ring today," she said. "Sally and I are happy to say that everyone is cleared for a trail ride this afternoon."

Maria gave Lizzie a high five. "Yes!" she said.

"Yes!" Lizzie echoed. She looked down at Jake, under the table. She'd passed! Trail riding would be great — she hoped — but she had a feeling that Jake would not be coming along. The truth was she would rather just stay back at the farm with this sweet, adorable puppy.

CHAPTER SEVEN

After lunch, Sally told the campers that they had an hour or so of free time before it was time to tack up again for the trail ride. "Maybe you'd like to head back to the river," she said. "The water's not quite warm enough for swimming yet, but it's nice for wading. Or you can relax on the porch, or play badminton — or help me with the dishes." She smiled as she said the last part.

Lizzie and Maria looked at each other. "Wading?" Lizzie asked. They both nodded. "Can Jake come with us to the river?" Lizzie asked Sally.

"Of course," she said. "He loves to splash around."

Lizzie and Maria helped carry dishes into the kitchen. They scraped the plates and stacked them on the counter. "Do you really want help?" Lizzie asked Sally, hoping that the answer was no.

"Thanks, sweetie," said Sally. "It's nice of you to offer, but Candace is here for that. You go on down to the river." She waved them away.

Lizzie and Maria and a few of the other girls headed down the path behind the barn, with Jake eagerly leading the way. He kept his nose to the ground, and his tail waved gaily as he sniffed.

I smell my friend! Maybe he's down here.

"Do you think he smells Smokey?" Lizzie asked.

"I'm sure he smells horses," said Maria. "Who knows if he can tell one from another?" She linked pinkies with Lizzie as they walked. "I'm so happy we get to go trail riding today," she said.

"So am I," said Lizzie. "Well" — she looked around to see if anyone could overhear — "happy, and maybe a little bit nervous, too."

Maria nodded. "I was nervous before my first trail ride, too. But trust me, you're going to love it. It's a whole different thing from riding in the ring. You see cool things, and you can smell all the forest smells, and the horses love it, too."

"I feel safe on Smokey," Lizzie said. "You were right about him. He's a total sweetheart."

"Told you," said Maria. "He was the first horse I ever rode here. He made me feel comfortable right away."

Ahead, the river sparkled in the sun. "I wonder if Jake knows how to swim," said Lizzie. "Maybe he'll jump in if we throw a stick for him." She watched Jake prance toward the moving water — then, suddenly, he veered off toward the big willow tree the same way Smokey had. "Look!"

Lizzie said to Maria. "He can tell where Smokey went!"

Jake snuffled along the path, wagging his tail harder than ever.

My friend was here! He went this way.

Maria laughed. "You're right," she said. "Smokey's the only horse who goes over there. I guess he and Jake really are besties."

Lizzie and Maria followed Jake to the willow and sat on a big flat rock beneath the tree's long dangly branches. It was cool by the river. A light breeze stirred the leaves on the trees. Jake splashed in the water where Smokey had slurped, then pranced back toward Lizzie with a big stick in his mouth.

"See? I bet he wants us to throw it in the river," Lizzie said as Jake dropped the stick at her feet.

She picked it up and tossed into the green water, and Jake leapt into the deeper part of the river, swimming hard with his nose lifted. "Go, Jake!" said Lizzie.

"He's such a strong swimmer," Maria said. "Look, he already got the stick."

Jake swam back, clambered up the riverbank, and ran toward Lizzie and Maria. He dropped the stick, then shook off, spraying them with cold water. "*Agghh!* Jake!" said Lizzie, but she couldn't help laughing. Jake looked so happy.

"Can Jake come with us?" Lizzie asked Sally later that afternoon. The horses were all tacked up and ready for their trail ride. Jake had stuck to Lizzie's side the whole time, exchanging kisses and snuffles with Smokey whenever he had the chance. Lizzie never would have dared to ask Jean, but maybe Sally would understand.

Sally shook her head. "No dogs on trail rides," she said. "We need to have our attention focused on the horses." She patted Jake's shoulder. "I know you'd love to come along with your friend," she told the gangly pup. "But we need you to stay here and guard the farm." Sally smiled at Lizzie. "That's what we've always told our dogs when we have to leave them home. Not that there's any need for guarding here. I just think it makes them feel better if they think they have a job."

Lizzie looked back at Jake as she and the other campers took off down the road, with Jean leading the way and Sally bringing up the rear. The brown-and-white puppy stood in front of the barn, Candace holding his collar, and watched them go. His long ears hung down, giving him a dejected look. Lizzie was sure Jake was feeling left out, and she promised herself to give him lots of attention when they got back.

The line of horses wended along the quiet country road for a few minutes. Then Jean turned her horse, Rocco, to the right, following a rutted trail through a wide meadow sprinkled with wildflowers in yellows, reds, and pinks. Lizzie took a deep breath. She loved the sweet smell of the grasses and flowers warming in the sun.

At the top of the meadow, the trail entered the woods through a gap in an old stone wall. Suddenly, all was cool and hushed, and the air smelled like Christmas trees as they rode beneath tall old pines. Under the horses' feet was a deep layer of pine needles; Lizzie could imagine how cushy it would feel to Smokey's hooves.

Nobody was talking. One horse followed another quietly through the forest. Shafts of sunlight found their way through the dark green branches, lighting their path. Lizzie felt as if she were in a fairy tale, the kind where a princess got lost in

the woods and came across a magical fountain —
a fountain with flowers all around it, and
maybe a unicorn grazing nearby. Lizzie wondered if Smokey would be friendly to a unicorn,
and decided that he would. Smokey was friendly
to everyone.

They crossed a stream and entered another
kind of woods, with tall maple trees towering
above and bright green ferns carpeting the forest
floor. Maria turned in her saddle to smile at
Lizzie, raising her eyebrows as if to say, "What
did I tell you?" Lizzie grinned back. Trail riding
was everything Maria had promised — and more.
The only thing that could possibly make it more
perfect would be a white dog with brown spots
running along next to Smokey.

CHAPTER EIGHT

Jake was waiting by the barn door when Lizzie and the other campers returned from their trail ride. He wagged his stumpy tail and let out a bark when he spotted Smokey.

Yay! My friend is back!

He followed Lizzie into the barn and stayed close while she removed her tack, brushed Smokey, and picked out his hooves. Lizzie noticed that having Jake nearby seemed to keep Smokey happy and calm, even while she was poking at the horse's big hooves or tugging at a knot in his mane. It was so sweet to see the friends enjoying each other's company.

After Lizzie turned Smokey out to pasture, Jake stayed with her while she mucked out Smokey's stall and added fresh new bedding, then cleaned out his water bucket and refilled it. Lizzie was getting used to the routine already. Even though it still felt like work to her, she was starting to understand why Maria thought it was fun. The girls laughed and talked as they did their chores. Jean seemed to trust them now; she poked her head into the barn only once, to tell them that dinner would be on the table "at six o'clock sharp."

Lizzie and Maria took another walk down to the river with Jake once they were done with chores, then hung out in the common room until dinner was ready. Lizzie almost fell asleep on the couch while they were waiting, and she could barely keep her eyes open during the meal. Still, she had the energy to join the others in a big cheer when Jean announced that the next day they would switch things up and start with their trail ride, saving the lessons for afternoon.

"Yay!" yelled Lizzie, along with everybody else.

"See?" Maria whispered into her ear a moment later. "Nothing to be nervous about, right?"

Lizzie nodded and gave her friend a fist bump. "Trail riding is the best," she said. "Let's see if we can do it at Kathy's sometime."

After dinner and cleanup, the campers sprawled in the common room to watch *The Black Stallion*. Some of the campers had seen the movie so many times that they could quote most of the lines. Lizzie had seen it only once, at Maria's house. She liked the movie, but as she lay on the couch with

Jake beside her, she kept drifting off, then waking with a start to find that she had missed another whole scene.

It had been a long, busy day at camp. Lizzie fell asleep the second her head hit the pillow, and she slept until Sally rang the breakfast bell, even though Jake took up at least half her bed. "You are such a bed hog!" she told him as she stretched and yawned, trying to wake herself up. Jake stretched, too, pushing his big blocky feet against her as he straightened his long legs.

I can take up even more space! Check this out.

"Hey!" Lizzie said as she fell out of bed with a thump. "No fair!" She jumped back on the bed to give Jake a hug, and he rolled over happily, ready for a belly rub.

This is the life! I get to be with my best friend all day and sleep in a comfy bed all night.

After breakfast and morning chores, Lizzie begged Sally again to let Jake come along on their ride. Sally shook her head. "It's not a good idea," she said. "Jake understands his boundaries here at the farm and won't run off, but if we head into the woods, he might decide to chase a rabbit, or poke his nose into a porcupine. We don't need the extra trouble."

Lizzie understood, but that didn't make it any easier to ride off on Smokey, leaving a lonely-looking Jake in the barnyard. "Bye," she called. "Be a good boy, Jake. We'll be back soon." Smokey turned back to look at his friend, too. He nickered softly, and Lizzie knew he was saying the same thing she'd just said, in animal language.

This time, Jean led them the other way

down the quiet road, then turned off onto a wide dirt trail Lizzie had not noticed before. "We'll trot a little today," Jean called. "Everybody ready for that?"

Lizzie felt butterflies in her stomach, but she swallowed hard as she nodded with everybody else. She took a deep breath and the butterflies went away. She leaned down to pat Smokey's shoulder. "Be nice," she said. "No galloping, okay?" That was her biggest worry: that a trot might turn into a canter and then a gallop. She did not like the idea of having her horse run away with her, taking off over the hills to who knew where. She trusted Smokey, though. He was steady and obedient, and there was no reason he would get it in his head to run off.

"Let's go," called Jean as she urged her horse forward. All the other horses began to trot. Lizzie nudged Smokey with her heels, and he picked up the pace. She posted, rising and falling in the saddle. They headed up the trail through tall grasses that rustled in the sunshine and gave off the delicious scent of warm hay.

Lizzie smiled to herself. This wasn't scary. This was fantastic. She felt like she could trot all day through this beautiful scenery. They passed a grove of white birch trees, bending gracefully like tall, slim ballet dancers. After that, they went by a rocky ledge covered in bright green moss. They splashed through a stream and rode along an old stone wall where apple trees bloomed pink and white, perfuming the air with their scent.

"Terrific, everyone," said Sally from behind as Jean slowed the pace. The horses went back to a walk as they emerged in a small grassy clearing. "Beautiful riding."

Lizzie relaxed into her saddle, feeling happy and alive. She bent to pat Smokey's neck again.

"Good boy," she murmured. Smokey tossed his head — then, suddenly, he let out a wild screech, a terrible sound, like none Lizzie had ever heard before. He tossed his head again and again, then rose on his back feet, bucking Lizzie off her saddle before she had a moment to wonder what was going on. She landed hard on the grass, letting out an "Oof!" as the wind was knocked out of her. And then, through the ground beneath her, she felt the thundering of Smokey's hooves as he galloped off — alone.

CHAPTER NINE

"Lizzie! Are you okay? Lizzie? Lizzie?"

Dimly, Lizzie heard Jean calling to her. She tried to answer, but her voice wouldn't work. Then she felt a hand on her forehead.

"Lizzie?" She recognized Sally's voice. The hand moved over her head, her arms, her legs. "Are you hurt anywhere?" Sally asked. "Does this hurt, when I touch you?"

Lizzie took in a deep, ragged breath. "I — I think I'm okay," she said. It wasn't easy to force the words out, but she managed. And it was true: she was okay. Nothing hurt — at least not too badly.

She wiggled one foot, then the other. They both worked. She tried her hands next. They worked, too. She opened her eyes. "I really think I'm okay. Is Smokey all right? What happened?"

"Bees." Sally was still checking Lizzie out. She touched Lizzie's head again. "So lucky that you were wearing a helmet. But did your head hit hard on the ground? Do you remember every-thing that happened?"

"Kind of," said Lizzie. "I mean, I fell off, right? When he reared? What do you mean, 'bees'?"

Sally nodded. "There's no way anybody could have stayed on. It was so sudden. I think Smokey must have stepped right into the nest of some ground bees. None of the other horses seem to have been stung."

Now Jean was kneeling by Lizzie's side, too. "Smokey was probably more frightened than hurt," she said. "He took off a mile a minute. But he'll come back. Horses are pack animals, and he'll want to be with his friends."

Lizzie sat up, with Jean and Sally both helping her. Sally felt all down Lizzie's back. "Nothing hurts?" she asked again.

"Nothing hurts," Lizzie said. "Well, maybe my elbow. But just a little."

"You'll have some pretty good bruises tomorrow," said Jean as she checked out Lizzie's elbow.

Lizzie looked around the small clearing where she sat. The other campers stared down at her from astride their horses. Maria's face was white. Lizzie gave her a thumbs-up and Maria smiled.

"The other girls did a great job," Jean said, loudly enough for everyone to hear. "They did exactly the right thing. Nobody panicked. Everybody stayed calm and paid attention to controlling her own horse. Excellent horsemanship, girls." She stood up and dusted off her hands. "We'll wait a little longer for Smokey to return. Then I'll lead us back down to the farm. Sally and Lizzie can follow, on foot if that's what works for Lizzie."

Lizzie was surprised. She sat up a little straighter and rubbed her elbow, which was definitely sore. "I thought you were always supposed to get right back on the horse after a fall," she said. "Isn't that what horse people say?"

"Some do," said Sally. "But we don't."

Jean shook her head. "It can be really scary when something like this happens. You might not be ready to ride right away, and that's fine. We never push any of our campers to do something that doesn't feel right to them."

Lizzie felt relief wash over her. She definitely was not ready to get back on Smokey — or any other horse. Not right now, and maybe not for a while. "I think I can stand up now," she said.

71

Sally and Jean each held one of Lizzie's arms as she rose to her feet. "Steady there," said Sally. "Okay?"

Lizzie nodded. "Okay." She peered into the woods that surrounded the clearing. "But what about Smokey? He's not back yet."

She saw Sally and Jean exchange looks. "He may have found his way back to the barn," said Jean. "That's happened before when a horse ran off. They know the way home, and that's where they want to be." Jean walked over to free Rocco's reins from the tree she'd tied him to. "We'll head back. You two take your time, and keep an eye out for Smokey."

"Will do," said Sally.

Jean put her foot in the stirrup and swung herself up onto Rocco's back. "See you soon," she said as she moved off, with the campers falling into line behind her. Last in line was Maria. She glanced back at Lizzie with a concerned look on her face.

"I'll be there soon," Lizzie called. She smiled and gave her friend another thumbs-up. "I'm fine. Really."

Maria grinned and waved. "I'll save you some lunch," she said as she rode off.

"Let's sit for just a few more minutes," said Sally. She plucked a blade of grass and twirled it in her fingers. "I remember the first time I fell off a horse," she said. "It was a pony, actually. My first pony. His name was Willy, and he looked a lot like a smaller Smokey."

Lizzie listened, grateful to be sitting still in the quiet clearing. "What happened?" she asked.

"I never really knew what spooked him," Sally said. "But he threw me just like Smokey threw you. I wasn't so lucky — I broke my wrist. But Willy and I went on to be good friends for a long, long time."

"Did you get right back on him after you fell off?" Lizzie asked.

Sally shook her head. "First my wrist had to heal, and then I had to get over my fear of it happening again. It took a while," she said.

"Did it happen again?" Lizzie plucked a blade of grass, too.

Sally laughed. "Oh, sure," she said. "If you have a life in horses, you're going to have those experiences. But I've never broken another bone." She got to her feet and dusted off her hands. "Ready to head back to the barn?" she asked.

Lizzie nodded. She took Sally's hand and stood up. Sally untied her horse's reins from a branch and gave him a pat on the neck. "Thanks for waiting, Boots," she said. Then they headed down the trail, Lizzie walking ahead of Sally, who led Boots. There was no sign of Smokey, but Sally assured Lizzie that he would be at the barn by the time they got back.

"Is he here?" Lizzie asked eagerly as she ran into the barn, her sore elbow forgotten. She was feeling fine, and she was ready to see Smokey, if not to climb on and ride him again.

Jean was pushing a wheelbarrow full of clean hay up the stable aisle. She shook her head, frowning. "No. Not yet, anyway. And somebody misses him big-time." She pointed to Smokey's stall. In front of it was Jake, sitting very still with a serious expression on his normally happy face.

Lizzie ran to Jake and knelt to put her arms around him. "Don't worry," she told the dejected puppy. "He'll be back."

CHAPTER TEN

Lizzie listened all through lunch for Smokey's hoofbeats or the jingle of his tack, but when the campers had finished their veggie burgers, the horse was still not back.

"We'll do some searching after lessons," Sally promised. "I still believe he'll find his way home. Meanwhile, we have another sweet horse you can ride if you want."

Lizzie shook her head. "I — I don't think I'm ready for that," she said. "Is it okay if I take Jake for a walk instead? He seems so sad. Maybe some activity will distract him from missing his friend."

Sally nodded. "Sure. Just keep him on a leash if you take him off our property. I don't want him chasing any critters in the woods or running into the road."

Lizzie promised she would take good care of Jake. She grabbed a leash from a hook by the door and went to find the puppy. It wasn't hard. He was still sitting in front of Smokey's stall. His ears were droopy and his head hung low.

Where's my friend? It's no fun around here without him.

"Jake!" said Lizzie. "Want to go for a walk?" She held up the leash, thinking that Jake would probably run over and jump on her in excitement. Jake just sat there. "Oh, well," said Lizzie. "You're going anyway. It'll be good for both of us."

She clipped the leash to his collar and they set off down the road. Lizzie thought she would explore a little, since she had two hours before lessons were over. But Jake had other ideas. His nose to the ground, he dragged her along the road, then abruptly left it, following the trail the horses had taken that morning.

My friend! My friend! He went this way!

At first Lizzie tried to tug Jake back to the road. "Where are you going?" she said. "Come on, Jake. This way." She really did not feel like revisiting the scene of her fall. Jake did not listen. He just pulled harder. That was when Lizzie realized how silly she was being. *Of course!* If anyone could find Smokey, it would be Jake. He had an incredible sense of smell, and he loved following his friend's scent. Lizzie spun around and let Jake tow her up the trail. He charged along, sniffing the ground wildly as he wagged his stumpy tail. Lizzie smiled. Here was a dog doing what he was born to do. It was a beautiful thing to see — if only he didn't pull her arm off!

They flew through the meadow with the long rustling grasses, then passed the beautiful white birch grove and the moss-covered rocky ledge. Jake didn't slow down at all as they splashed across the stream. He dragged Lizzie behind him as he galloped along the old stone wall, kicking up fallen apple blossoms as he ran.

Lizzie began to have a queasy feeling in her stomach as they entered the clearing where Smokey had stepped on the bees' nest. "Slow down, Jake," she said. She pulled back on the leash, but it was no use. Jake kept charging along, straight through the clearing. Lizzie barely had time to remember the awful moment when she'd been thrown to the ground. Now Jake was off the trail, leaping over fallen trees and pulling Lizzie through rough underbrush. Lizzie felt her excitement growing. Would Jake really find Smokey?

The question was answered almost immediately. After they'd gone only a little way into the dense woods, Jake began to whimper. The whimpers turned to whining and then to joyous barking.

There he is! I knew it! I knew it!

Sure enough, there was Smokey. He tossed his head and nickered when he saw Jake and Lizzie. "Smokey!" said Lizzie. She ran to him and threw her arms around his neck without a moment's hesitation. Poor Smokey. His reins were tangled in a mass of prickly branches. Lizzie saw scratches on his nose from the long thorns. She wondered if

Smokey knew how strong he was. Surely, if he had pulled hard enough, the reins or the branches would have broken. But he just stood waiting, and his patience had paid off. His friend had found him.

Jake danced around at Smokey's feet, reaching his neck up for kisses and whimpering with happiness.

I'm so happy to see you, my friend!

Lizzie reached in, trying to get the reins untangled without scratching herself too badly. She tugged and pulled, pushing the branches back with her other hand, until the reins came loose from the tree. Then she stood there for a moment. *Now what?*

She knew that she could walk Smokey all the way back to the barn, just as Sally had walked

Boots. She could take his bridle in her right hand and walk just ahead of him, leading him back to the farm. But she didn't want to do that. She wanted to get Smokey back home, and she wanted get there as quickly as she could so that Sally and Jean would know he was safe and sound. That meant riding him.

Somehow, Lizzie's fear of getting back on a horse had disappeared. She could do it; she knew she could. But how could she get on by herself, without a leg up? Smokey was so tall! Lizzie wished she could put one foot in a stirrup and swing herself up the way Jean did it, but the stirrup was way too high for her to reach.

She looked around. *There!* A stump, just the right height. If she stood on it . . . Within a few seconds, Lizzie was astride Smokey's back, settling into the saddle and picking up his reins, ready to ride. Lizzie's heart thumped wildly for a moment, but she pulled herself together.

With Jake at their side, Lizzie and Smokey pushed through the dense woods. Lizzie steered the gray horse carefully through the clearing, avoiding the spot where he'd stepped on the bees' nest, then along the stone wall, across the stream, past the rocky ledge and the birch grove, and finally down the trail through the long rustling grasses. She beamed with pride as she rode up the road toward the farm.

"Look who we found!" she called to Sally, who was in the riding ring, giving Maria a lesson.

"Lizzie!" cried Maria.

"Smokey!" said Sally.

Riding lessons ended as everyone clustered around Lizzie, Smokey, and Jake. Jean helped Lizzie slide off Smokey as Sally knelt to hug Jake.

"Nicely done," Jean said quietly to Lizzie after Lizzie spilled out the whole story. "You really used your brain and your riding skills. I'm proud of you."

Lizzie felt her eyes fill with tears. Maria threw her arms around Lizzie and hugged her tight. "You are awesome!" said Maria.

"Jake is awesome," said Lizzie. "He's the one who found Smokey. He did it all. I think he deserves some really good treats."

"I think he deserves more than that," said Sally. "I think he deserves to stay with his friend forever." She looked at her cousin. "What do you say? Shall we keep him?"

Jean raised her eyebrows. Then she nodded. "I have to admit that he's shown some potential as a barn dog," she said. "He's a fast learner, and Lizzie's done a great job helping him calm down. Anyway, how can I say no after he found Smokey?"

Lizzie and Maria hugged each other again. How incredible was this? Jake had found the best forever home in the universe, the perfect one for him. "Yay!" yelled Lizzie before she remembered about not shouting around the horses. She put a hand over her mouth, but Jean just smiled at her.

"You and Jake have both convinced me that you have a place here at Appletree Farm," Jean said. "I hope you'll join us this summer for a whole week. You'd be great with some of the less experienced campers."

Lizzie didn't know what to say. "Wow, thanks," she replied. "I'd love to." Suddenly, she couldn't wait. She'd get to see Jake again and ride Smokey and muck out stalls and haul water. Maria was right. Horse camp was the best.

PUPPY TIPS

As Lizzie learned, taking care of horses can be a lot of work and a big responsibility. Every type of pet has its own needs. If you decide to get a puppy or a cat, or a bunny or a lizard, or a goldfish or a hermit crab, it's up to you to learn how to take good care of your new friend. When we take animals into our homes and our lives, they depend on us for all their needs. What kind of food does your pet need? How much water? What type of home or environment? How much exercise? You can learn from a friend, from a teacher, from a book, or from the Internet. And don't forget that your pet needs plenty of love and attention from you, too!

Dear Reader,

My dog Zipper is part German shorthaired pointer, so it was fun to write about Jake. Zipper loves to sniff and snuffle through the woods, picking up the scent of every other creature that has passed that way. Sometimes I wonder if he could find me if I were lost in the forest. He probably could, as long as he didn't get too distracted by chasing squirrels!

He has never met a horse, but I wouldn't be surprised if he got along fine with a pony like Smokey. Zipper is a friendly guy who likes everybody he meets, which is one reason I love him so much.

Yours from the Puppy Place,

Ellen Miles

THE PUPPY PLACE

DON'T MISS THE NEXT PUPPY PLACE ADVENTURE!

Here's a peek at BITSY!

"Mom!" Charles yelled. "Mom, wait!"

But it was too late. She had already pushed her shopping cart through the supermarket's second door, which was sliding shut behind her.

Without even thinking, Charles pulled the sign off the bulletin board and ran after her. "Mom!" he called, waving it in the air.

She was waiting for him by the soda-can return

machines. She pulled two bags of groceries out of the cart and nodded to the third one. "Can you carry that?" she asked.

He held up the sign. "I will, but can you just look at this?"

"Charles," Mom said. "These bags are heavy. Let's get the groceries into the car, then you can show me."

Charles pulled the last bag out of the cart and followed Mom to the van. She slid the back door open and loaded her bags of groceries into the way back seat. Charles got in with the bag he was carrying and buckled himself in, trying hard to be patient.

Finally, Mom got into the driver's seat. She turned around. "All right," she said. "What was it you wanted me to see?"

Charles held up the sign. "This," he said.

"Whoa, that is one tiny puppy!" said Mom.

Charles grinned. "I know. Isn't she the cutest puppy ever?" He turned the sign back his way so he could look at it again. The puppy in the picture looked a lot like Princess, a Yorkshire terrier the Petersons had once fostered: she had long, silky brown hair, perky ears, and shiny brown eyes. The difference was in size. Princess had been a small puppy and would probably never grow very large. But this puppy was smaller than small. This puppy was teeny-tiny, barely bigger than a hamster. In the picture, she was posed inside a red high-top sneaker. The sneaker had glittery red laces, and the puppy wore a matching red bow on the top of her teeny-tiny head.

Mom raised an eyebrow. "I wonder why she's looking for a new home," she said.

"I don't know, but we have to help her," said Charles. One look at this dog's picture had